Katie Kazoo,
SWITCHEROO

All's Fair

Katie Kazoo, SWITCHEROO

All's Fair

by Nancy Krulik • illustrated by John & Wendy

Grosset & Dunlap
An Imprint of Penguin Group (USA) Inc.

GROSSET & DUNLAP
Published by the Penguin Group
Penguin Group (USA) Inc., 375 Hudson Street,
New York, New York 10014, USA
Penguin Group (Canada), 90 Eglinton Avenue East, Suite 700,
Toronto, Ontario M4P 2Y3, Canada
(a division of Pearson Penguin Canada Inc.)
Penguin Books Ltd, 80 Strand, London WC2R 0RL, England
Penguin Ireland, 25 St Stephen's Green, Dublin 2, Ireland
(a division of Penguin Books Ltd)
Penguin Group (Australia), 707 Collins Street,
Melbourne, Victoria 3008, Australia
(a division of Pearson Australia Group Pty Ltd)
Penguin Books India Pvt Ltd, 11 Community Centre,
Panchsheel Park, New Delhi—110 017, India
Penguin Group (NZ), 67 Apollo Drive, Rosedale,
Auckland 0632, New Zealand
(a division of Pearson New Zealand Ltd)
Penguin Books (South Africa), Rosebank Office Park, 181 Jan Smuts Avenue,
Parktown North 2193, South Africa
Penguin China, B7 Jiaming Center, 27 East Third Ring Road North,
Chaoyang District, Beijing 100020, China

Penguin Books Ltd, Registered Offices:
80 Strand, London WC2R 0RL, England

Text copyright © 2013 by Nancy Krulik. Illustrations copyright © 2013 by John & Wendy.
All rights reserved. Published by Grosset & Dunlap, a division of Penguin Young Readers Group,
345 Hudson Street, New York, New York 10014. GROSSET & DUNLAP is a trademark of
Penguin Group (USA) Inc. Printed in the U.S.A.

Library of Congress Control Number: 2012012074

ISBN 978-0-448-45682-9   10 9 8 7 6 5 4 3 2 1

ALWAYS LEARNING   PEARSON

For Jeffrey and Amy, for reasons known
only to them—NK

For Sarah, Shane, Kate, Katie,
Bonnie, Netta, and all the good friends
the magic wind has blown our way—J&W

Chapter 1

"You can do it!" Katie Carew cheered as her friend Jeremy Fox threw a rubber-tipped dart at the target she had set up in her backyard.

Plop. The dart missed the target and landed in the grass.

Jeremy frowned, but Katie kept smiling.

"That's the closest you've gotten yet!" she told him.

Jeremy shrugged. "Yeah, but I still missed," he said. "I'll never win a prize at the Cherrydale County Fair."

"Sure, you will. You're getting much better," Katie assured him. "Besides, the fair's not until this Saturday. You still have a whole week to practice."

"Not really, Katie Kazoo," Jeremy said, using the way-cool nickname Katie's friend George had given her back in third grade. "I've got a soccer game tomorrow and a drum lesson on Tuesday. Then there's my travel team soccer practice on Wednesday and—"

"Ruff! Ruff!"

"Woof! Woof!"

Just then, Katie's chocolate and white cocker spaniel, Pepper, came racing across the lawn with a dart in his mouth. Pepper's best friend, Snowball, was following right behind him.

Jeremy reached down and took the dart from Pepper. "Man, that's slimy," he said. "Who knew dogs had so much spit?"

Pepper looked up at Jeremy and wagged his tail. He was very proud of himself. He'd just fetched the dart and brought it back.

"Thank you," Katie said, bending down and petting the soft, smooth fur on Pepper's head. "Good dog." She looked up at Jeremy. "You want to try again?"

Jeremy wiped the slimy dog spit off the dart with the bottom of his shirt. "Definitely," he said.

Jeremy pulled his arm back and got ready to throw. But before he let the dart go, a loud screeching noise came from the yard next door.

"*You are my sunshine, my only sunshine. You make me happy . . .*" Katie's neighbor, Mrs. Derkman, was singing at the top of her lungs.

"*Aroooooo!*" Snowball howled along.

"*Ruff! Ruff!*" Pepper joined in.

"Mrs. Derkman must be gardening again," Katie said. "She says singing makes her roses grow larger."

"That's not singing," Jeremy said. He shook his head. "I still can't get used to the fact that our old teacher lives next door to you."

Mrs. Derkman had been their third-grade teacher last year. She was the toughest teacher in the whole school. Katie was glad she was in fourth grade with Mr. Guthrie now. He was the coolest teacher in the whole school. Mrs. Derkman wasn't exactly what anyone would call cool.

"You'll never know, dear, how much I love you . . . ," Mrs. Derkman sang out.

"Aroooo!" Snowball howled.

"Um . . . Katie, you want to practice in my yard for a while?" Jeremy suggested. "It's hard to concentrate here. Besides, Lucky doesn't fetch. It will be easier to throw a dry dart than a slimy one."

Lucky was Jeremy's pet cat. "Okay," Katie said. She picked up the target. "Just let me tell my dad where I'm going."

★ ★ ★

*"Daisy, Daisy, give me your answer do.
I'm half crazy over the love of you . . ."* Mrs.
Derkman squawked . . . er . . . *sang* to her
rosebushes as Jeremy and Katie walked to
Jeremy's house.

"Hi, Mrs. Derkman," Katie said. "Your roses
look really pretty."

"Yes, my babies are getting there," Mrs.
Derkman said. "But they're not quite big
enough to win a blue ribbon at the county fair.
I wish we had a few more weeks, so they could
really blossom."

Katie stopped dead in her tracks and stared
at her neighbor. "YOU DO NOT WISH THAT!"
she exclaimed loudly. "YOU CAN'T!"

Mrs. Derkman lifted the brim of her green
gardening hat and stared strangely at Katie.
"Why not?"

Katie gulped. Why not? Because people
should never make wishes, that's why. Wishes
were dangerous things. Especially if they came
true. And no one knew that better than Katie
Kazoo.

Chapter 2

It all started one day at the beginning of third grade. Katie had lost the football game for her team, ruined her favorite pair of jeans by falling in the mud, and let out a gigantic burp in front of the whole class. It was the worst day of Katie's life.

That night, Katie had wished she could be anyone but herself. There must have been a shooting star overhead, because the very next day, the magic wind came.

The magic wind was like a wild tornado that blew just around Katie. She never knew when the wind would arrive, but whenever it did, her whole world was turned upside down. That was because the magic wind was so powerful it could turn Katie into someone else. One . . . two . . . switcheroo!

The first time the magic wind came, it turned her into Speedy, the third-grade class hamster. While Katie was Speedy, she'd spent the whole morning running around, trying not to get stepped on.

The magic wind returned later to switch Katie back to herself. But it wasn't finished with her. The wind had been back plenty of times since then. Like the time it turned her into Lucille, the lunch lady at school. Katie had started a food fight and had almost gotten Lucille fired.

Another day, the magic wind came and switcherooed Katie into a hairdresser named Sparkle. Katie didn't know the first thing about cutting hair, so just turning into a hairdresser would have been bad enough. What made it worse was that Katie's best friend, Suzanne Lock, was the person getting her hair cut. Boy, did Katie make a mess out of Suzanne's head!

And then there was the time the magic wind switcherooed Katie into a baseball player named Mike Reed. Mike was an awesome shortstop. But Katie wasn't. She dropped a really important fly ball—and then started to cry in front of a whole stadium of fans. Only the fans didn't know that it was a fourth-grade girl who was crying on the jumbotron screen. They thought it was Mike. That had been *sooo* not good!

That was the problem with the magic wind. Every time it came, it made a mess of things, and Katie was left having to fix everything. That one little wish had gotten Katie into heaps of trouble. So she didn't make wishes anymore. And she didn't like when anyone else did, either.

Of course, Mrs. Derkman didn't know that. *Nobody* knew. Katie had never told anyone about her switcheroos. She couldn't. No one would believe her. Katie wouldn't have believed in switcheroos, either—if they didn't keep happening to her.

Still, Katie had to tell Mrs. Derkman something. So she said, "I just mean, your flowers are almost perfect. If you had to wait longer than a week, they might start to wilt. Or bugs could get at them."

Mrs. Derkman made a face at the word *bugs*. She hated all insects. "You're right!" Mrs. Derkman exclaimed. "Bugs are the enemy! I have to go to the store and get more insect repellant."

And with that, Mrs. Derkman got up and headed right for her scooter, which was parked in her driveway. "I'll see you kids later," she said as she put on her helmet. "I must protect my babies."

"Come on, Katie," Jeremy said as soon as Mrs. Derkman sped off. "I need to practice. This year I'm going to win a prize even if I have to spend *all day* throwing darts in the midway."

Chapter 3

"Okay. On your marks! Get set! EAT!"
Kadeem Carter shouted in the cafeteria during
lunch on Monday. He clicked the button on his
stopwatch.

Almost immediately, Andrew Epstein began
shoveling his lunch in his mouth. He ate his
sandwich in just two bites and swallowed a
whole carton of milk without ever putting it
down.

"Gross," Suzanne said. She put her lunch
tray down next to Katie's. "What are they
doing?"

"I'm timing Andrew for the pie-eating
contest they're having at the county fair,"

Kadeem told Suzanne. "He has to eat two whole pies faster than anybody else."

Suzanne watched as Andrew stuffed a handful of grapes into his mouth. His cheeks puffed out like a squirrel eating nuts.

Just then, Mrs. Derkman came over to the lunch table. "Andrew, slow down," she warned. "You're going to choke if you're not careful."

"But—" Andrew began to say.

"And don't talk with your mouth full!" Andrew shut his mouth, chewed, and slowly swallowed. "That's better," Mrs. Derkman told him and walked away.

"Man, she's still being bossy and she's not even our teacher anymore," Kevin said as soon as Mrs. Derkman was out of earshot. "I pity the third-graders who have her."

Katie pulled her sandwich from her lunch bag, looked at it, and shook her head. "More blueberry jam," she said with a sigh.

"Don't you like blueberry jam?" Emma Weber asked her.

"Sure," Katie said. "It's just that my mom and grandma have been making batches and batches of it for weeks now. They're trying to get it perfect so they can win a blue ribbon at the fair. I'm their official taster." She took a bite of her sandwich. "I think this is from batch forty-seven."

"All I have for lunch is cold leftover pizza," Emma said. "My mom has no time for cooking or baking. She says that with five kids she should get a prize just for getting through the day."

Katie smiled. Emma's mom was probably right. Especially since two of those kids were Timmy and Tyler, her wild two-year-old twin brothers.

Kevin Camilleri pulled a giant red tomato out of his bag. "Have you guys ever seen a tomato this big?" he asked the other fourth-graders.

"Are you going to eat that whole thing?" Jeremy asked.

"Definitely," Kevin said. "And I have cherry tomatoes for dessert."

"How many does that make, Kevin?" Katie asked him.

Kevin pulled a pad from his back pocket and wrote down a number. "I have eaten six hundred twenty-seven tomatoes since the beginning of the year," he announced.

"Too bad they don't have a blue ribbon for that," Emma Stavros said.

"Yeah." Kevin agreed. "But they do have a prize for the biggest, reddest, roundest tomato. And I'm going to win that. My dad has been helping me grow them in the little greenhouse that we built. Every one I've grown is as beautiful as this one right here."

"Hey, do you guys know how to fix a broken tomato?" Kadeem asked, looking up from his stopwatch.

"How?" Kevin wondered.

"Tomato *paste*!" Kadeem laughed at his own joke.

"That's pretty good," Kevin said with a laugh. He looked over at Andrew. "You missed a peanut butter cracker," he told him.

"Thanks!" Andrew said with his mouth full. Little bits of bread, cracker, grapes, and peanut butter flew out of his mouth.

"No talking!" Kadeem yelled at him. "You have to swallow every bite."

"That's disgusting," Suzanne said.

Becky Stern looked across the table at Jeremy and batted her eyelashes. "Are you going to win a prize for me this year?"

"If I win anything, I'm keeping it," Jeremy told Becky.

"Well, maybe you'll win an extra prize that I can have," Becky replied.

"It seems like everyone is entering something at the fair," Emma said.

"Not me," Katie told her. "I just want to go see the farm animals. Maybe I'll get to milk a cow or pet a pig."

"Eww, I'm not getting near them!" Suzanne

said. "I'd get all smelly, and Miss Candy Apple has to smell sweet, not yucky."

"Miss who?" Katie asked her.

"Miss Candy Apple," Suzanne repeated, loud enough so everyone could hear her. "Well, *Junior* Miss Candy Apple, actually. It's a beauty pageant. I'm sure I'll win. After all, I *am* a model."

"No, you're not," Mandy Banks told her. "You're just a kid who takes modeling classes."

"It's the same thing," Suzanne insisted. "And I'm ready. I've been practicing my beauty pageant face for weeks now." She tilted her head to the side, smiled, and shoved her fingertips into her cheeks.

Kadeem also puffed up his cheeks, tilted his head, and pushed his fingers into his face. All the air rushed out. He sounded like a balloon that had popped. "Maybe I'll enter, too," he said. Jeremy and Kevin laughed.

"*Here he is, Mr. Candy Apple*," Jeremy sang.

Kadeem got up and started walking around the table, waving to everyone like a beauty queen. "That's *Junior* Mr. Candy Apple," he said, correcting Jeremy.

"Go ahead, make fun," Suzanne said. "But I'll be the one having the last laugh at the fair when I win the title. And believe me, I *will* win."

Chapter 4

"Watch me wave one more time," Suzanne told Katie as the girls arrived at the Cherrydale County Fair on Saturday morning.

"Suzanne, I've been watching you wave, walk, and smile for almost a whole week now," Katie reminded her.

"Come on, girls," Katie's mother said excitedly as she and Katie's grandma hurried through the parking lot. Katie's mother held a jar of their homemade blueberry jam.

Katie picked up the pace. She was excited, too. This week had gone by so slowly—with Katie watching Suzanne walk and wave, helping Jeremy with dart throwing, and taste testing oceans of blueberry jam. But finally, here she was at the fair— Katie couldn't wait to get on the rides, see her friends, and play with the animals.

"Do you know what time Downhill Slide is playing?" Suzanne asked.

Katie looked at her, surprised. Downhill Slide was a band. Their music teacher, Mr. Starkey, performed in it. Suzanne had never cared about the band before.

"At twelve o'clock," Katie said.

"Oh good!" Suzanne said. She sounded really excited. "I want to be there just in case any of the pageant judges are around. I want them to see me dancing. I want them to notice how much I love everything about this fair. Junior Miss Candy Apple has to be beautiful *and* have a sparkling, winning personality."

As they reached the gate, Katie's mom turned to them. "We're going over to the food tent," Mrs. Carew told Katie and Suzanne. "The jam judging is at twelve thirty if you want to stop by."

"Oh, I'll be there," Suzanne assured her. "I'm going to make sure I'm seen at everything."

"Don't you mean you're going to make sure you *see* everything?" Katie's grandma asked her.

"Oh. Yeah, right," Suzanne said. But Katie knew Suzanne had meant what she said the first time.

Katie started to walk through the gate and onto the fairgrounds. But Suzanne stopped her short.

"Wait a minute," Suzanne said. She pulled a big tube of glitter out of her pocket and rubbed some in her hair and on her cheeks. "There. That's better. I couldn't walk into the fair unless I was all shimmery. You want some?"

Before Katie could even answer, Suzanne squealed and said, "*OOOOH.* That guy over there is selling candy apples! Here. Keep this for me." She shoved the tube of glitter in Katie's hand. Then she ran off, leaving Katie all by herself.

Katie wasn't alone very long, though.

A moment later, she spotted Emma and her brother Matthew coming toward her. Katie waved to them. "Hi!" she said. "Where are you guys heading?"

"To get a teddy bear!" Matthew said excitedly.

"My mom gave me some money to try and win prizes," Emma explained. "You want to come?"

"Sure," Katie said. "The goat milking isn't for a while."

"What celebrity is milking them this year?" Emma asked her.

"An old-time rodeo cowboy named Slim Jim McQueen," Katie replied.

Matthew's eyes opened wide. "A real, live cowboy?"

Katie nodded.

"Oh, Em, we gotta see him!" Matthew exclaimed. "After I win a prize," he added.

"Yum!" someone said really loudly.

Katie turned around. It was Suzanne.

"This candy apple is scrumptious." She took

another bite. "And extra sticky, too."

"Why are you talking so loud?" Emma asked her.

"Was I?" Suzanne asked. "I guess it's just all my excitement at eating this DELICIOUS CANDY APPLE."

Katie knew Suzanne was talking that way to make sure people noticed her. But Katie didn't mind. It was just Suzanne being Suzanne.

Just then, Emma's older sister, Lacey, came over with Tyler and Timmy. The twins were bouncing up and down like little jumping beans. Lacey looked worn out. "You take them," she said to Emma.

Before Emma could argue, Lacey grabbed Matthew by the hand. "And, oh, I almost forgot. I entered you in the Junior Miss Candy Apple Contest!"

Emma's eyes shot open wide. *Almost as wide as Suzanne's did.*

"You didn't!" Emma and Suzanne shouted at the same time.

"You're just the right age," Lacey said.

"But I don't like beauty pageants," Emma said.

Suzanne nodded. "Yes! Beauty pageants are awful."

Katie stared at Suzanne. Where was this coming from?

"If you don't have a chance at winning," Suzanne continued.

"What's that supposed to mean?" Emma asked.

"Well, you know, *I'm* in the contest," Suzanne said sweetly. "And I'm a professional model. So you don't stand a chance."

Emma thought about that for a minute. Then she smiled at Lacey. "Thanks for entering me."

"Suit yourself," Suzanne told Emma. "But you're making a big mistake, isn't she, Katie?"

Uh-oh! Katie didn't know what to say. This Junior Miss Candy Apple Contest was turning into one very sticky situation.

Chapter 5

Katie, Suzanne, Emma, and her brothers entered the tent where the pie-eating contest was being held.

"Want pony ride," Tyler whined.

"We will go to ride the ponies," Emma promised Tyler, "right after we watch my friend eat pie."

"No pie!" Tyler shouted. "Ponies!"

"Yes! Ponies!" Timmy added.

"Ponies! Ponies! Ponies!" the twins chanted.

Emma looked like she had a bad headache.

Andrew and the other contestants were seated at a big picnic table. Two huge pies were in front of each of them.

"There he is!" Katie shouted excitedly. She stood by Kadeem. "I don't how he is going to be able to eat all that in one minute!"

"He's trained really hard," Kadeem reminded her.

"Good luck, Andrew!" the girls shouted.

"You can do it, buddy!" Kadeem cried.

Just then, someone blew a whistle and the contest began. Katie watched as Andrew started shoving huge handfuls of blueberry pie down his throat.

"Okay, that's just gross," Suzanne said. "Why doesn't he use a fork?"

"Being neat takes too much time," Katie told her.

Now Andrew's whole face was in the pie. He was making loud slurping noises.

"Look! He's almost finished one pie," Kadeem cried. "All that training sure came in handy."

"It looks like half the pie is on his clothes. And his face is all purple with blueberry juice," Suzanne said.

"See that guy on the far right?" Emma pointed out. "He's on his second pie."

"Go, Andrew!" Katie cheered as Andrew shoved another huge fistful of pie into his mouth and began to chew. Pieces of blueberry dribbled out of the corners of his mouth and onto his shirt.

"This is so boring," Suzanne said with a yawn. She took a big bite of her apple. "*Mmmm.* Delicious!"

"I wanna candy apple!" Tyler shouted.

"Me too!" Timmy echoed.

"Mama already said no candy apples," Emma told them. "They're terrible for your teeth, and you guys bounce off the walls when you have a lot of sugar."

"*Mmmm.*" Suzanne took another bite of her apple, licked her lips, and smiled at the twins. "This is just about the best candy apple I've ever eaten!"

"Candy apple! Candy apple!" the twins began chanting. "Candy apple!"

Suzanne took another bite. "That's right," she said. "This is my candy apple! *Mmmm . . .* good."

Tyler and Timmy looked like they were going to cry.

"Suzanne! Cut it out!" Katie and Emma said at the same time.

Katie sighed and looked back at the pie eaters. "Andrew and that guy on the far right are both almost finished."

"It's gonna be close," Kadeem agreed. "Come on, Andrew. Chew that last big piece!"

Andrew opened wide and shoveled in more.

"Andrew! Andrew! Andrew!" Emma and Katie cheered.

"Candy apple! Candy apple!" the twins screamed.

"Oh no!" Katie said. The guy at the other end of the table swallowed his last piece before Andrew had finished chewing. And that meant he was the winner. Andrew was in second place.

Kadeem looked very upset.

Andrew looked like he might throw up. "All that training. All that eating. All for nothing."

"Second place is great!" Katie said.

"Candy apple! Candy apple!" Tyler echoed.

Emma sighed. "I told you. No candy apples. How about I get you two guys a nice pretzel?" She looked down and gulped.

Uh-oh! Instead of two guys, there was only one.

"Oh no!" Emma exclaimed. "Timmy's gone!"

This was *soo* not good.

Emma started to cry.

"Don't worry, Emma," Katie said, wrapping her arm around Emma's shoulders. "He can't have gone far. We'll help find him."

"Me?" Suzanne asked. "Why should I help?" Suzanne started to walk away.

Katie thought fast. "Wait, Suzanne! If you find Timmy, you'll be a hero," Katie said. "I bet beauty pageant judges love heroes!"

Suzanne turned and smiled broadly. "Well, what are you waiting for?" she asked Katie and

Emma. "We have to rescue Tyler!"

"Timmy," Katie corrected her.

"*Whatever*," Suzanne said. "Let's just find him!"

Chapter 6

"We should look for a policeman," Katie said after the guy at the candy apple cart said he hadn't seen Timmy.

"I don't see any," Suzanne said. "Let's go to the midway. All little kids want those stuffed animals."

"It's worth a try," Emma agreed. Emma was holding Tyler's hand tight. She wasn't about to lose two brothers.

At the midway, Katie went up to a young guy running the balloon-dartboard booth. "Excuse me," Katie said. "Have you seen a little boy who looks exactly like this one?" She pointed to Tyler.

"Huh?" the guy asked. "Why would you be looking for this kid if you've got him right here?"

"Not him," Suzanne said. "His twin brother."

"Oh," the guy said. "Nope. Sorry."

Suzanne frowned and took another bite of her candy apple. "Well, I'm all out of ideas," she said.

"I wanna go see the aminals like Timmy!" Tyler shouted out suddenly.

The girls all looked at him.

"What did you say?" Emma asked her brother.

"I wanna go see aminals like Timmy," Tyler repeated. "Ride a pony!"

"That's it!" Katie exclaimed. "Timmy went looking for the ponies at the petting zoo."

Emma picked Tyler up so she could run faster.

At the petting zoo, there were lots of people around the pens. A gazillion little kids were petting the bunnies, feeding the goats, and

riding on the ponies. How were they ever going to find Timmy in the crowd?

Suzanne wrinkled her nose. "It stinks around here."

Suddenly Emma shouted, "There he is!"

"Where?" Suzanne asked her.

"Over by the baby chicks!" Emma said. She started to hurry over to her little brother.

"Wait!" Suzanne insisted, pushing Emma out of the way. "I'll get Tyler."

"Timmy," Katie corrected her.

"Timmy! Stay right where you are!" Emma shouted. "I'm coming!"

Suzanne began shoving her way through the crowd. "Coming through," she called. "There's a lost boy who needs rescuing."

Ooomf! A little girl ran right into Suzanne.

Boom! Suzanne fell backward and landed in a pile of straw.

"OH NO!" she shouted. "The candy apple is stuck in my braid!"

"Hold still," Katie said. She yanked the

candy apple out of Suzanne's hair.

"Ouch!" Suzanne cried. Then she scowled and looked at the candy apple Katie handed her. "Yuck! I don't want it now. It's got hair on it. Thanks a bunch!"

Emma walked over with Timmy and Tyler. Emma looked exhausted. But the twins were full of energy.

"Can I have a candy apple now?" Timmy asked.

"Me too?" Tyler wondered.

"No candy apples," Emma said with a sigh.

"How about a nice pretzel?"

"Yuck!" Timmy said.

"We want candy apples," Tyler added.

"When I'm Junior Miss Candy Apple, I'll make sure you get some," Suzanne told them.

Emma glared at her. "Who says you're going to win?"

"I say," Suzanne told her. "And I'm always right. Aren't I, Katie?"

Katie didn't know who was right. In fact, all she knew for sure was that this Junior Miss Candy Apple Contest was never going to end *apple-y* ever after!

Chapter 7

Katie was glad when Emma went off with her brothers for a pony ride and Suzanne headed to the bathroom to fix her braid. That gave Katie a little time to be alone. She decided to go back to the midway and see what prizes you could win.

Jeremy was standing near the balloon dartboard.

"I'm trying to decide whether to try this game again," Jeremy told her. "A minute ago I almost won."

"Yeah, kid, you nearly did," the guy behind the counter said. "Try again. I bet you'll win a prize this time. Come on, a quarter a dart. Four for a dollar."

"I don't know . . . ," Jeremy said. "I don't have a lot of money left."

"You were really good in my backyard," Katie reminded him.

"I guess," Jeremy said. He reached into his pocket and plunked a quarter on the counter. "One dart please."

"Attaboy," the guy behind the counter said. He handed Jeremy a dart.

Jeremy squinted his eyes and aimed the dart at one of the balloons pinned to a white board about twenty feet away. The dart zoomed toward the board.

Katie watched excitedly. Jeremy had really good aim. His dart was headed right for a yellow balloon in the center row. It flew closer and closer and . . .

PLOP. The dart seemed to bounce off the balloon before falling to the ground.

"Hey! That dart hit the yellow balloon!" Jeremy said.

"Definitely," Katie agreed.

"It couldn't have," the guy behind the counter told them. "If a dart hits a balloon, the balloon pops. It must have just been so close that it *looked* like it hit the balloon."

Jeremy frowned. "See what I mean?" he asked Katie. "This game is really, really hard. And I should know. That was the fifth time I tried it."

"I could have sworn you hit the balloon," Katie told him.

Jeremy shrugged his shoulders. "At least I got rid of Becky. She got tired of watching me lose."

Katie laughed. That was Jeremy. Always looking on the bright side.

"I'm hungry. I'm going to get myself some fried dough," Jeremy said. "You want to come?"

Katie shook her head. "I'm going over to watch the celebrity goat milking. They have a real cowboy—a rodeo star—there today."

"Cool," Jeremy said. "But do me a favor, will you?"

"Sure, what?"

"If you see Becky, don't tell her where I went," Jeremy said.

* * *

A big crowd was gathered around the livestock area where the celebrity goat milking was being held. There were photographers and reporters from the local newspapers. A lot of the little kids were wearing cowboy hats. Some of the older kids were holding autograph books. It seemed like everyone wanted to see a real, live rodeo cowboy up close.

Katie walked over to where some goats were penned, waiting to be milked or entered in the livestock contest. Suzanne was right about one thing: Even Katie had to admit that the goats *did* smell.

It was quiet near the pens. The goats were all just standing there, happily chewing on oats. They weren't arguing or complaining. They knew exactly how to enjoy a county fair!

Katie walked over to a cute goat with a brown face, long white ears, and a soft brown-

and-white beard. "Hello," she said.

Splat! Katie looked down. Oh no! She had stepped in a big pile of goat poop. One of the goats must have gone to the bathroom before being put in the pen. *Grrr.* This day was definitely not turning out the way Katie had expected.

"Couldn't you learn to use a toilet or a litter box or something?" Katie shouted at the brown-and-white bearded goat.

"*Maaaaa,*" the goat answered her.

Katie started scraping the bottom of her sneaker against a piece of wood. As she tried to get the poop off, she felt a cool breeze blow gently against the back of her neck. Her red hair began to blow into her eyes.

That was strange. The goat's fur wasn't blowing. Neither were the oats and hay. Everything was still. There wasn't wind blowing anywhere . . . except around Katie. Which could only mean one thing. This was no ordinary wind. This was the *magic* wind! Oh no!

Oh *yes*!

The magic wind began to blow more and more wildly, until it was circling Katie like a fierce tornado. The wind was so powerful, Katie thought she might be blown away! She shut her eyes tight and tried really hard not to cry.

And then it stopped. Just like that. The magic wind was gone. And so was Katie Carew. She'd been turned into someone else. One . . . two . . . switcheroo!

But who?

Chapter 8

The smell was awful. That was the first thing Katie noticed when the wind finally stopped blowing. Wherever she was, it stunk really, really bad.

Katie was afraid to find out where that awful magic wind had blown her this time. But she opened her eyes, anyway, and looked around.

To the left were two goats. One was pale white with just a hint of brown on her tail. The other was brown and white with huge, thick horns. They were both standing quietly in a pen, chomping on hay.

Phew. That was a relief. Katie hadn't been

blown far away. She was still at the county fair. Okay, so now Katie knew *where* she was. But she still didn't know *who* she was. What she did know, though, was that she was starving. Too hungry to even think! And for some reason, she had the strangest desire to chomp on one of Mrs. Derkman's roses. But there were no roses in sight. So Katie lowered her head and began to chew hay, taking care not to get any caught in her small, white beard. Yummy! The hay was fresh. There was nothing tastier than fresh hay.

Just then, an annoying fly landed right on the small of Katie's back.

"Get off me," Katie bleated. "Can't you see I'm eating?" She bent down and grabbed another piece of hay with her mouth. She chewed for a minute and then stopped.

Hey, wait a minute. Tail? Hooves? Beard?

Fourth-grade girls didn't have any of those. At least not any fourth-grade girls Katie had ever met. But *goats* had them. And that could only mean one thing: Katie had turned into a goat. Right here in the middle of the Cherrydale County Fair!

Katie took another bite of hay and chewed. She was definitely hungry. Katie had always thought nanny goats ate garbage—anything from leftover food to tin cans. At least that's what she'd always seen in cartoons. But right now, Katie wasn't looking for a trash can to have her lunch. What she was really in the mood for was a picnic lunch of flowers.

"Maaa! Maaa!" Just then, one of the goats

began bleating from her pen.

"*Maaa! Maaa! Maaa!*" Some of the other goats bleated back.

Katie had goat feet, goat eyes, goat fur, and a goat beard. But Katie did not *speak* goat. Still, it wasn't hard to understand what these goats were saying. They were very excited. Someone they knew was coming near the stalls.

"*Maaa! Maaaa!*" the billy goat bleated happily.

A tall man in jeans with big, heavy boots walked toward Katie's pen. "Come on, Maybell," he said as he gently wrapped a rope around Katie's neck like a leash. "Lunch is over. It's milking time."

Chapter 9

The farmer led Katie up some stairs to a wooden platform that had been set up in the middle of the petting zoo. He stroked Katie's neck gently and placed a bucket underneath her. A moment later, a second goat walked up the stairs and onto the platform with another farmer.

"*Maaa . . . Maaa . . . ,*" the other goat bleated to Katie. But she couldn't speak goat.

Katie looked around. Down below the platform she could see big pens set up everywhere. There was a pen with three bunnies to her left. Another pen with two lambs was on her right. There were piglets in a pen beside the lambs. And in the middle was a big pen filled with little yellow chicks.

But no one was paying attention to those baby animals now. They were all too busy staring at the stage.

The two farmers walked over to the microphone and smiled at the crowd. "Welcome to the celebrity goat-milking contest," one of the farmers said. "I'm Farmer Gene Greens, and this is my goat, Maybell. She's here and ready to be milked."

Katie knew that was true. Her belly felt very full. *"Baaa!"* she said.

"I'm Farmer Stan Kornblatt. And this is my goat, Velma," the other farmer said. "She's ready to be milked, too!"

"Maaaaa," Velma bleated.

"We have a real rodeo cowboy here to show you just how much fun it is to milk a goat," Farmer Greens continued. "Slim Jim McQueen!"

Slim Jim leaped up onstage and waved his

hat in the air. The crowd cheered.

"I bet y'all are wondering why we have two goats," Slim Jim said. "It's because I am challenging someone from this audience to a goat-milking race! Is there anyone here who thinks they can fill a bucket with fresh goat's milk quicker than I can?"

"I'LL DO IT!"

A shout came from the middle of the crowd. Katie recognized the voice right away. She'd know it anywhere. The voice belonged to Suzanne!

Suzanne jumped up onto the platform. She smiled at the crowd and took a bite of another candy apple.

"What's your name, little lady?" Slim Jim McQueen asked her.

"I'm Suzanne Lock," she told him. "And I'm a fashion model." She turned sideways, looked over her shoulder, and posed for an imaginary photographer.

"Do you know how to milk a goat?" Farmer

Greens asked
Suzanne.

"Sure,"
Suzanne said.
"I've milked a
million of 'em!"

Katie shook
her hairy head.
"That's a lie!"

she shouted out. But the only thing the crowd
heard was, *"Maaa. Maa. Maaaaaa!"*

"So you really think you can beat Slim
Jim?" Farmer Kornblatt asked her.

"I'm sure going to try." Suzanne peered at
the crowd. "I try my hardest at whatever I do!
So how about a round of applause for me?"

A few people started clapping.

Katie was confused. Suzanne had made it
clear she didn't want to be around any animals.
But now here she was volunteering to milk
goats.

"And after you all take lots of pictures of

me milking this goat, please come see me in the Junior Miss Candy Apple Contest," Suzanne continued.

Oh. *Now* it made sense. No matter what the smell, Suzanne always had to be wherever the action was—especially if there were photographers and cameras around.

But that didn't make it okay. The last thing Katie wanted was for Suzanne to milk her. Still, Katie wasn't worried. Wouldn't Farmer Greens want a grown-up to milk his goat? He was probably going to shoo Suzanne right off the stage.

"Great, Suzanne," Farmer Greens said. "I like your spirit. Why don't you just take a seat right here next to Maybell?"

Katie's goat eyes opened wide. She couldn't believe her big, floppy goat ears.

"Thank you," Suzanne answered. She started walking toward where Katie . . . uh . . . *Maybell* was standing.

There was only one thing to do. Katie leaped

off the platform and into the crowd. It was time
for this goat to make a run for it!

Chapter 10

"Uh-oh! Maybell's on the loose!" Farmer Greens shouted into the microphone.

"I'll lasso her!" Cowboy Slim Jim McQueen announced. He picked up a rope from the stage, tied a loop at the end, and began spinning it in the air. "Yeeehaw!" he shouted.

"Yahooooo!" the people in the crowd cheered.

"Out of my way!" Katie shouted, racing through the petting zoo. All that came out was *"Maaa! Maaaa!"*

"Oink! Oink!" the pigs shouted angrily as Katie banged into the pigpen.

"Sorry," Katie bleated.

"Yeehaw!" Slim Jim shouted again.

His lasso whirled in the air.

"Oh gosh!" a woman cried. "The chicks have escaped!"

The circle of the lasso flew out toward Katie's head.

"*Cheep! Cheep! Cheep!*" The chicks clucked as they ran in all directions.

"Chicks on the loose!" a little kid shouted.

Katie ran from the lasso as fast as her goat legs could carry her.

"Watch out for the chicks!" Farmer Greens yelled into the microphone.

"I've got one!" someone shouted.

"Me too!" a teenage boy said. "Fast little guys, aren't they?"

"Helloooo!" Suddenly Katie could hear Suzanne's voice calling out on the microphone. "Have you all forgotten there's a fashion model with a candy apple up here?"

But nobody was paying attention to Suzanne while there were baby chicks on the loose. In a flash, Katie managed to scoot out of the petting zoo and across the midway. She had no idea where she was going. But she had to get out of there!

The next thing she knew, Katie was inside a crowded tent. Katie sniffed the air. *Mmmm. Flowers.* They smelled so sweet and delicious.

"Oh, Freddy Bear, I hope I win the blue ribbon," Katie heard a woman say. "Do you think the judges really liked my roses?"

It was Mrs. Derkman and her husband. Mrs. Derkman was wearing a big straw hat with fake flowers on it.

Suddenly, Katie's goat tummy started rumbling. She was still hungry. And all those roses looked delicious. Not the fake ones on Mrs. Derkman's hat. The real ones. There wasn't another goat around, so it was like being the only customer at a yummy bouquet buffet. *Roses, tulips, daffodils, pansies . . .*

Even though she was a goat, Katie knew she should get away from the flowers. She should sneak back to the stalls and munch on some straw and oats. But those flowers looked so yummy. She couldn't help herself.

Katie chomped off a couple of Mrs. Derkman's red roses. *Gulp!*

"EEK!" Mrs. Derkman yelled. She ran over and yanked at the stems hanging from Katie's lips.

"What is that goat doing in here?" a judge demanded.

"My babies!" Mrs. Derkman cried. "That rotten goat ate my babies! Somebody grab it!"

"I'm sorry," Katie bleated. Then she took off.

But all Mrs. Derkman heard was *"Maaaa. Maaaa."* And, boy, was Katie's neighbor *ma-a-ad*!

Suddenly, everyone in the flower tent was racing after Katie. It was a good thing Katie had four legs. She could run twice as fast as any two-legged human. And at least no one here had a lasso!

Katie kept running. And running. And running. When she finally stopped, she was in a small parking area. There were a few trailers, a water hose, and a big stack of hay. Overhead, a big banner read WELCOME FARMERS. It was where the farmers unloaded the livestock, but it was empty now.

Katie stopped to rest. Almost right away, she felt a cool breeze blowing against her furry back. She looked around. The hay in the haystack wasn't moving at all. The banner overhead wasn't moving, either. The breeze was only blowing on Katie. And it was getting stronger by the second.

That could only mean one thing. This wasn't an ordinary wind.

This was the magic wind. It had come back!

This time, Katie was *glad* the magic wind was blowing. Katie was tired of being a goat. This four-legged kid was ready to go back to being a two-legged kid.

The magic wind began to pick up speed. It whirled and swirled all around Maybell— uh, er, *Katie*—like a wild tornado. It blew through her fur like a hurricane, raising her tail in the air and flapping at her ears. Katie shut her goat eyes tight and tried to keep herself from being blown away.

And then it stopped. Just like that. The magic wind was gone.

Katie opened her eyes and looked down. Sure enough, her four hooves had disappeared. In their place were two human feet in red high-top sneakers.

Woo-hoo! Katie Kazoo was back!

And so was Maybell the goat. She was standing there, right next to Katie. Boy, did she look confused.

Chapter 11

"Poor Maybell," Katie said. She stroked her
back gently. "You must be tired and thirsty
after all that. I know I am."

"*Maaaaa*," Maybell bleated.

Katie had a feeling Maybell was saying
yes. So she got up, turned on the hose, and let
Maybell drink from the stream of cold water.

"That's a good girl," Katie said, using the
same kind of voice she used when she spoke to
Pepper.

Maybell looked up at her. "*Maaaaa . . . ,*"
she said again. Then she shook her head. A
few drops of water flew out of her beard and
sprayed Katie.

"Okay, I guess I deserved that," Katie said. "I'm sorry I ran off like that, but I didn't want you . . . I mean, I didn't want me . . . well, I didn't want Suzanne milking either of us."

Maybell had no idea what Katie was saying. But something in Katie's voice seemed to soothe her. She sat down in the haystack and began nibbling.

"You sure are a mess." Katie reached over and gently began smoothing Maybell's fur. She was soft and fuzzy.

"*Maaa. Maaa,*" Maybell bleated.

"Where is my goat?"

Suddenly, Katie heard Farmer Greens shouting. It sounded like he was coming her way.

He definitely sounded upset. And he thought Maybell was all to blame.

"She's got a lot of spirit," Katie heard someone answer. It sounded like Slim Jim.

"Too *much* spirit," the farmer replied. "I don't trust her near people anymore. I may just have to sell her."

"Maybe Maybell's back in the livestock tent," Slim Jim said.

"It's worth a look," Farmer Greens said.

Then Katie heard the farmer and cowboy walk off. They never even spotted Maybell and Katie.

Katie gulped. *Sell* her? Farmer Greens couldn't do that. His farm was Maybell's home. All her friends were there.

This was *sooo* not good!

"I have to do something to make that farmer

like you again, Maybell," Katie whispered quietly.

Maybell chewed some more hay. She had no idea what was going on.

Usually Katie had great ideas that could fix the messes the magic wind made. But not today. That was the problem with great ideas. Like the magic wind, they only came when they wanted to.

✦ ✦ ✦

Katie shoved her hands in her pockets and leaned against a post. Suddenly she felt something wonderful in her hand—Suzanne's container of glitter. That was it!

"Maybell!" Katie announced. "You're entering a contest!"

Quickly, Katie picked the gravel from Maybell snowy white beard. Then she smoothed out her soft fur and fluffed up her tail.

"Okay, now for the sparkle." Katie sprinkled Suzanne's shimmery pink-and-white glitter all over Maybell's furry body. "Pageant judges love glitter. At least that's what Suzanne says."

Katie stood back and looked at Maybell. Now her fur sparkled in the sunshine.

"Come on," Katie said as she placed her hand on Maybell's back and led her over to the livestock area. "Let's hope this works."

"Maaa. Maaa!"

The other goats greeted Maybell. They sounded really glad to see her.

Farmer Greens looked at Katie. Then he looked at Maybell. "What's going on here?"

"I found your goat," Katie said.

"Well, you shouldn't have brought her here," the farmer said. "This is a contest to judge the best-looking goat at the fair. Maybell's a troublemaker. She can't be trusted at a judging. She's liable to bolt again. And what's that in her coat?"

"Glitter," Katie said. "It's what girls wear in pageants."

The farmer frowned. "Maybell's not a girl. She's a goat. And this isn't a beauty pageant. It's a contest for dairy goats. The judges look for things like height and weight, the shape of her ears, and how well-groomed her fleece is."

"She's very well-groomed," Katie assured him. "I pulled every bit of gravel I could find out of her beard."

Farmer Greens frowned. "Gravel in her beard? How did she manage to do that?"

Katie watched as the judges walked over to a brown-and-white goat. They placed their hands on the goat's ribs and studied the shape of her ears. Then they marked something down on a card and walked over to a white goat with small horns. That goat was pretty. But she didn't look as nice as Maybell did.

"Maybell looks beautiful," Katie insisted. "Give her a chance. I think she'll behave now."

"What makes you such an expert on goats?" Farmer Greens asked.

Katie wasn't sure how to answer that. Luckily, she didn't have to. At just that moment, the contest judge walked over to Farmer Greens.

"And who is this lovely goat?" the judge asked.

"She's . . . uh . . . ," Farmer Greens stammered. "Well . . . "

"She's Maybell," Katie interrupted. "She's a last-minute entry into the contest. She's not too late, is she?"

"Not at all," the judge said. "Is she yours?"

Katie shook her head. "No. I'm just a friend. She belongs to Farmer Greens here." Then she held out her hand. "My name is Katie."

The judge shook Katie's hand. Then he began to walk all around Maybell. He looked at her fluffy tail and admired her beard. "Nice goat! Her legs are spaced well," the judge remarked. "And her back looks straight and strong."

Katie smiled. So far, so good. Even Farmer Greens seemed to be relaxing—at least a little.

Then the judge brought another judge over to look at her. "Her coat is very thick and shimmery," the first judge said, writing something on his pad.

Shimmery was exactly the look Katie was going for.

"We're ready to announce the winners," one of the judges said a few minutes later. They headed straight over to a farmer who was standing beside a pretty white goat. The farmer was handed a white ribbon. That was for third place.

Then the judges walked over to a black-and-gray goat. She got a red ribbon for second place.

"Uh-oh!" Farmer Greens said. "That was Stan Kornblatt's goat that just got second place. Stan's never going to let me live this down. His goats always beat my goats in contests."

Katie had only been trying to help. "I'm really sorry," she apologized.

And then, the judges came over and stopped right in front of Katie and Farmer Greens. "This goat is magnificent!" one declared.

"Her ears are perfectly shaped, and she's got wonderful bone structure. Her fur is shiny, and she is clearly well-groomed. Congratulations! Here's your first-place blue ribbon. This goat is best in show!"

The crowd clapped loudly. Farmer Greens's jaw dropped. He stared at the judge. He was so surprised, he couldn't even speak.

So Katie took the ribbon and thanked the judge.

"You're welcome, little lady," he replied.

Farmer Greens looked at Katie. "I guess I owe you an apology," he said.

Katie grinned. She was actually the one who owed him an apology—for running off the platform and for letting all the chicks loose in the petting zoo and for eating Mrs. Derkman's roses. Of course, he didn't know about the roses.

But he might in a minute. Mrs. Derkman was heading in their direction. Katie gulped. If Mrs. Derkman told the judges what Maybell had done, they might take away her first-prize ribbon.

"*Maaaa. Maaaaa,*" Maybell bleated.

"Um . . . she looks really uncomfortable," Katie said quickly. "Maybe she needs to be milked."

Farmer Greens nodded. "Yes. We need to get her back to the pens."

"Yeah, right away," Katie agreed.

Off they hurried. Mrs. Derkman never spotted them! *Phew!*

"Oh, can I milk Maybell?" Katie asked Farmer Greens. "I've always wanted to try that."

"Sure," he answered. "Let me get you a bucket. And then I'll show you exactly what to do. It's the least I can do after all you did for us. Imagine! Maybell won a blue ribbon!"

"So you're not going to sell her?" Katie asked.

"I would never sell Maybell," Farmer Greens said. "She's going to make me rich."

"How?" Katie wondered.

"Just think of all the goat cheese I can sell using her milk," Farmer Greens said. "Can't you just see the advertisements? Blue Ribbon Goat Cheese."

Katie giggled. "I like it."

"*Maaa. Maaaa,*" Maybell bleated. Obviously she liked it, too.

Chapter 12

"Katie, where have you been?" Suzanne demanded a little while later when she spotted Katie at the band shell dancing to the music of Downhill Slide. Their music teacher, Mr. Starkey, was the drummer. And he was awesome.

"I was . . . I . . . uh . . . I made a new friend," Katie said finally. There. That was the truth, sort of.

"Your new friend isn't entered in the Junior Miss Candy Apple Contest, is she?" Suzanne asked.

Katie shook her head. "No."

Suzanne looked relieved. "You sure missed a

lot of excitement. Some goat went nuts, and it was terrible."

"Terrible?" Katie asked. She hadn't thought things were that bad.

"The milking contest had to be canceled," Suzanne went on. "Everyone had their cameras out, ready to take pictures of me milking a goat, and then the goat took off. Once all the chicks got loose, people had to settle for taking pictures of the chicks instead of me."

"I'm sure they were all disappointed," Katie said with a laugh.

"Oh, definitely," Suzanne agreed. "How often do you get a picture of a fashion model milking a goat?" She stopped and turned her head as something caught her eye. "Oh, look, there's another candy apple stand," Suzanne said. "I'm going to buy another."

"How many have you eaten already?" Katie asked.

"I don't know. Three. Maybe four," Suzanne replied. "They're delicious. You want one?"

"No, thanks," Katie said. "I want some funnel cake." She went over to the snack stands. "One funnel cake, please," she said to the man behind the counter. Then she noticed Kadeem and Andrew. They were sitting on a bench nearby.

"Oh . . . please don't say the word *cake*," Andrew said to Katie.

Andrew still had purple berry juice all over his shirt and pie crumbs in his hair. He had undone the top button on his jeans, and he was clutching his stomach.

"Andrew's not feeling so great," Kadeem told Katie.

"Too much pie?" she asked Andrew and Kadeem.

"Definitely don't say *pie*!" Andrew moaned.

"Not enough pie," Kadeem corrected Katie. "Or he might have won."

"Those other guys were a lot taller and a lot bigger. And the guy who took first place has been in a lot of eating contests. He won a hot

dog contest in New York once."

"Ooooh," Andrew said, doubling over. "Don't say *hot dogs*."

Just then, Suzanne wandered over with a shiny, red candy apple. "I think this is the sweetest candy apple I've ever tasted," she said loudly. Then she took a huge bite.

"Oooooh," Andrew said. He got up from the bench. "I need a bathroom."

"Was it something I said?" she asked Katie.

"More like something Andrew ate," Katie assured her.

"All that pie," Suzanne said knowingly.

"Exactly," Katie agreed. "I'm going over to see how my mom and grandma are doing. You want to come?"

Suzanne nodded. "Definitely. I want to see everything at the fair," she said loudly and then looked around to make sure lots of people had heard her. "I have real county fair spirit! And that's the kind of spirit you need if you're going to represent the fair as Junior Miss Candy Apple!"

Katie laughed. Suzanne was definitely one of a kind.

"You girls are just in time," Katie's grandmother greeted Suzanne and Katie. "They're about to taste our jam."

Katie's mom crossed her fingers. "Wish us luck."

Katie crossed her fingers, too.

As the two judges walked over to the table, Suzanne gave them a big smile. "Hi, judges," she said. "I guess you're here to taste this delicious jam."

"Yes, we are," one of the judges said.

"Is this the only contest you judge?" Suzanne wondered.

"No. We also judge the cake contest," the other judge told her.

"Oh, just another food contest," Suzanne said. She stopped smiling. "Never mind then."

The judges didn't say anything as they tasted the blueberry jam. Then they put down their spoons and moved on to the next contestant.

"Did they seem to like it?" Katie's mother asked.

"I couldn't tell," Katie's grandmother replied.

"Do you think we should have gone with batch twenty-eight?" Katie's mom wondered.

"Too late now," her grandmother said.

As Katie stood there with her mom and grandmother, she could tell they were both nervous. They had worked so long to make the perfect jam. Everyone else looked nervous, too, waiting to see who would win that blue ribbon.

The judges pulled out their packet of ribbons. They walked past Katie's mom and grandma to a table to the right and handed a white ribbon to two gray-haired ladies who had made strawberry jam.

"Okay, that means we didn't come in third," Katie's mom said.

"Or second," Katie's grandmother added. "They just gave the red ribbon to that guy who made the boysenberry jam."

Katie had never heard of a boysenberry jam before. She wondered if there was such a thing as *girls*enberry jam, too.

But there was no time to ask. Because at just that moment, the judges started walking back toward where Katie's mom and grandma were standing.

"They're coming this way," Katie's mom said excitedly.

Katie crossed her fingers tighter. "Please . . . please . . . please . . . ," she whispered quietly.

"And the blue ribbon goes to the blueberry

jam!" one of the judges announced. He handed Katie's grandma a blue ribbon.

"YESSSS!" Katie, her mom, and her grandma all screamed at once.

Suzanne just stood there biting her candy apple. She looked bored—until the fair photographer appeared at the table. "I'd like to get a picture of the winners with their jam," she said.

"Come on, Katie," Katie's mom said. "You helped, too. You should be in the picture. This is a family affair."

Suddenly, Suzanne was *very* interested. "I'm practically one of the family," she told the photographer as she pushed her way into the photo right between Katie and her grandma. "Come on, everyone. Say *candy apple!*"

Chapter 13

"Make a basket, win a balloon!" A carnival barker in a red-and-white-striped Cherrydale County Fair shirt was shouting. Suzanne had gone off to fix her hair and put on more glitter. That left Katie to wander around on her own.

"Come on, girlie," the barker at the get-a-Ping-Pong-ball-in-the-milk-bottle booth called to Katie. "Three tries for a dollar."

"No, thank you," Katie said. She wasn't very good at carnival games. And she really wasn't interested in winning the little rubber doll prizes at the Ping-Pong ball booth.

Katie didn't want to spend her money trying to win plastic rings at the duck pond booth

or felt hats at the water balloon–race booth,
either. In fact, there wasn't a prize at the
midway Katie would have wasted her money
trying to win, except for the stuffed animals at
the balloon-dartboard booth.

But it looked as if nobody had won one,
because she didn't see a single person walking
around with a big stuffed bear or cat.

Just then, Katie ran into Jeremy. "Hi, Katie," Jeremy greeted her.

"Hi. Guess what! My mom and grandma just won first prize for their jam!" Katie said excitedly. She smiled at his big felt hat. "Oh! You won a water balloon race!" she added happily.

"Yeah," Jeremy said. "I wanted to win a stuffed animal, but it's impossible. I think that dartboard game is rigged."

"Hey, try your luck again, kid!" the guy behind the balloon-dartboard booth shouted to Jeremy. "We got big prizes here!"

"Yeah, I know. But what are the chances of me winning one? Zero?" Jeremy said. Then he faced Katie again. "That guy just stands around shouting all day."

Katie looked at all the giant prizes hanging from the ceiling of the balloon-dartboard booth. They sure were cute.

"I'm going to go see how Kevin and his tomatoes are doing," Katie told Jeremy. "You want to come?"

Jeremy shook his head. "I'm going to try to knock down those milk bottles with a baseball. They have inflatable shark prizes there. It's not a stuffed bear, but it's something."

"Okay, well, good luck," Katie said. "See you later."

As Katie exited the midway, she turned left. But a minute later she realized she had definitely gone the wrong way. There were no mechanical bulls here. No rides. No games. No people. And no tomatoes. In fact, there wasn't anything here except big crates and boxes and two huge garbage dumpsters.

This was not where Katie wanted to be. It was a very creepy feeling being all alone by the garbage area. And those dumpsters really stunk—even worse than the goats had smelled earlier. Quickly, Katie turned around and started to retrace her steps.

Katie shivered a little. She wished she had a warmer jacket with her, but the day had been so warm before, she hadn't bothered to bring one.

It was getting windy, too. Katie wrinkled her nose, expecting the gross smell of the garbage to following her in the wind.

But Katie didn't smell anything. That was because the wind wasn't blowing around the dumpsters or the crate boxes or anywhere else. In fact, the only place the wind was blowing was around Katie.

Katie knew that could only mean one thing. This wasn't any ordinary wind. This was the magic wind.

"Not again!" Katie shouted at the magic wind. "You were just here. Can't you leave me alone?"

But the magic wind didn't hear anything Katie said. Or if it did hear, it didn't care. It picked up speed and started circling around Katie like a wild tornado. Around and around the wind blew. The wind was so powerful, Katie felt like it was lifting her way off the ground. She shut her eyes tight and tried not to cry.

And then it stopped. Just like that. The

magic wind was gone.

But so was Katie Kazoo. She had turned into someone else. One . . . two . . . switcheroo.

But who?

Chapter 14

Katie sniffed at the air. The stench of garbage dumpsters was completely gone. It had been replaced with the scent of popcorn, candy apples, and funnel cakes.

Slowly she opened her eyes and looked around. There were the knock-down-the-milk-bottles game booth and the booth where you blew up a balloon with a water gun. Wow! This time the magic wind had been so powerful it had swept Katie right off her feet and carried her back to the midway.

Okay, so now Katie knew *where* she was. But she didn't know *who* she was.

Katie looked down. Her red high-top

sneakers had been replaced by brown boots. And she wasn't wearing her sweater and skirt anymore. Now she was wearing brown shorts. Yuck! Her legs were so hairy—almost like a goat's. But there were only two of them. And they were definitely human legs.

Katie was also in a red-and-white-striped official Cherrydale County Fair shirt and a name tag that read GILBERT. Which had to mean that the magic wind had switcherooed her into Gilbert. But *who* was Gilbert?

Just then, a big guy who was also wearing a fair T-shirt stomped over to Katie. "Yo, Gil! What's the matter with you?" he asked.

"Huh?" Katie murmured.

"I haven't seen one mark here at the dartboard booth in the past ten minutes," the big guy said. "We should have customers swarming to this booth. Now start calling, or I'll send you to the boneyard."

Katie gulped. She didn't understand anything the big guy had just told her.

Still, she had figured one thing out. Obviously, this Gilbert guy was a carnival barker. Which meant now *Katie* was a carnival barker. And it was her job to get people to come throw darts at the balloons in her booth.

"Pop a balloon! Win a prize!" Katie shouted. "Win a stuffed toy! Four darts for a dollar!"

"That's more like it!" the big guy said and walked away. But no one stopped at Katie's booth. So she shouted a little louder. "Come on, folks. Throw some darts, win a bear!"

A teenage boy and his girlfriend stopped at Katie's booth.

"Which bear do you want, Shana?" he asked.

"Oh, the blue one, Frank," she answered.

"You got it," Frank said. He handed Katie a dollar. "Give me four darts, please."

"Sure," Katie said.

"Frank's a really talented dart thrower," Shana told Katie. "Get ready to give me that blue teddy bear!"

Katie smiled and handed Frank four darts.

His first three shots missed completely. But the fourth one . . .

"Hey! That one hit the red balloon," Frank told Katie. "I'm sure of it. So how come it didn't pop?"

Katie was thinking the same thing. It sure looked like the dart had hit the balloon. But she had to be wrong. After all, the balloon didn't pop. And like Gilbert had told Jeremy earlier, if the dart had hit the balloon, it would have popped for sure. Wouldn't it?

"Want to try again?" she asked.

"Are you kidding? No one can win at this game. Come on, Shana, let's try something else," Frank said.

As they walked away, Katie pulled the darts from the board. "Pop a balloon! Get a bear!" she shouted.

"If you don't start earning some alfalfa soon, Carl is gonna kill you." The guy in the booth next to her patted the money pouch he wore around his waist. "I've been raking in the green, and all I'm giving away is plastic jewelry."

Katie looked at him strangely. *Alfalfa? What does that mean?*

"He's not kidding," the guy across the way at the ski ball booth agreed. "You better fill that possum gut by the end of the day."

Possum gut? Katie was really confused. She didn't see any possums anywhere. Maybe they were off eating some of that alfalfa. This job wasn't nearly as easy as Katie had thought. You practically had to learn a whole new language just to work here.

"Possum gut?" Katie asked.

"Yeah, you know, your cash register," he said, looking at Katie as if she'd lost her mind. "Which had better be filled with alfalfa by the time Carl gets back."

Katie nodded. She guessed alfalfa meant money. After all, that was what people *usually* put in a cash register.

"Gil, I thought Carl was gonna fire you on the spot before," the skee ball guy told Katie.

Katie didn't need a dictionary to figure out what that meant. Obviously, Carl was the big guy who had come by to yell at her. The skee ball guy was right. Carl had been pretty angry.

Katie looked around the booth. There were plenty of balloons tacked onto the board. So there were lots of chances for someone to win. The only thing was, when you looked closely, you could see the balloons hadn't been blown up all the way. Katie thought they would look so much prettier if the balloons were blown up really big.

Katie reached under the counter and yanked out a bag of fresh balloons. She pulled a yellow one from the bag and blew it all the way up. She knotted the end nice and tight and pinned it to the board. Then she did the same with an orange balloon.

A few minutes later, there were ten bright, new, shiny balloons pinned to the board—and Katie was completely out of breath. Now she'd better get customers and put some alfalfa in her possum gut. Otherwise, Carl would send her to the boneyard—wherever that was.

"Pop a balloon, win a prize!" Katie shouted loudly to a tall man who was carrying a little girl on his shoulders. "Come on, pal, be a hero.

Win a teddy bear for the little girl."

"Please, Uncle Joe," the little girl said. "I need a new teddy bear."

"You *need* one, Ella?" Uncle Joe asked.

"Well, I want one, anyway," Ella said.

"Okay, I'll give it a try." The man lowered Ella to the ground and plunked a dollar on the counter.

"Here ya go," Katie said in her best carnival barker voice as she handed him four darts.

Joe picked up a dart and aimed. Then he let the dart go. It sailed across the booth, heading for the board. And then . . .

Pop!

All the air rushed out of the green balloon.

"You did it!" Katie shouted. She jumped up and down and clapped her hands with glee. *Oops.* That didn't sound like a real carnival barker. Katie smiled. "Um . . . I mean . . .WE HAVE A WINNER!" she said.

"I want the yellow bear," Ella said.

"Here you go," Katie said, taking the bear

off the shelf. "Now, who's going to be the next winner?"

A teenage girl said she'd try. On her third dart, a balloon popped. Off she went with a blue kitten.

The next thing Katie knew, there was a line at her booth. Balloons were popping. Prizes were practically flying off the shelves. She had to blow up more balloons. And the *possum gut* was filling up with dollar bills. Katie was really proud of herself.

Pop!

Pop!

Pop!

"GIL, WHAT'S GOING ON HERE???"

Just then, Carl came bounding over to Katie's booth. And he did not look happy.

Chapter 15

"Who changed the balloons?" Carl asked Katie.

"I did," Katie answered proudly.

"Excuse us, folks," Carl said. "This booth is closed for a few minutes. Go try another game." Then Carl grabbed Katie by the arm. "Are you nuts?" Carl asked once he was sure no customers could hear him. "Nobody is *supposed* to pop those balloons. The way they are now, they pop too easily."

Katie stared at him. "But if they don't pop, people can't win."

"Well, *duh*," Carl said. "You have the most expensive prizes in the whole midway at your booth. The cheap prizes I can afford to give away. But not these."

Katie's eyes opened wide. Jeremy had been right. The balloon dartboard was rigged to make it really hard for people to win. "But that's not fair," she told Carl.

"It's fair to me," Carl told her. "And if you want to keep your job, you'll put those squishy balloons back on the board."

"I'm no cheater," Katie told him.

"It's not cheating. It's just making it harder to win," Carl said. "Besides, the people are here to have fun playing the games. They don't really care if they get a prize."

Katie knew that wasn't true. People wanted to win. That was the whole point.

"Look, Gilbert, I don't know what your problem is," Carl continued, "but a million people want this job if you don't."

Katie doubted that. Being a barker wasn't nearly as easy or fun as she thought it would be. All that shouting to get customers had left her throat raw. And it was tough standing around all the time. Plus, having a boss like Carl was horrible.

"I ought to charge you for those prizes," Carl shouted.

Katie couldn't take being yelled at anymore. She might have looked like a grown man named Gilbert, but she was really just a ten-year-old girl named Katie. And so she did a very ten-year-old girl thing. She started crying and ran away.

The dumpsters still stunk, but now Katie didn't care. At least this was one place she could be alone. Nothing could stink worse than listening to Carl. Poor Gilbert. He sure did have it rough.

Just then, Katie felt a cool breeze blowing against the back of her neck. She looked around. The wind didn't seem to be blowing anywhere else. Which could only mean one thing. The magic wind was back!

Just like before, Katie wasn't upset to feel

that wild tornado start churning around her. In fact, she was glad. The sooner the magic wind turned her back into Katie Kazoo, the better!

The magic wind picked up speed then. It whipped around her so hard, Katie thought she might be blown right out of the fairgrounds and into the next county! She closed her eyes tight.

And then it stopped. Just like that. The magic wind was gone. And Katie Kazoo was back!

But so was Gilbert. He was standing there, right next to Katie. And boy did he look confused!

Gilbert sniffed at the air and wrinkled his nose. "What am I doing back here by the dumpsters?" he asked Katie. " And who are you?"

"I'm Katie," she said.

"I'm Gilbert." He introduced himself.

"I know," Katie said.

"How?" Gilbert asked her. "Have we met?"

Oh yes! But Katie wasn't about to explain

all about the magic wind and switcheroos to Gilbert. He'd never believe her, anyway. So instead she said, "It says so on your name tag."

"Oh, yeah, right," Gilbert said. "I'm a little confused right now. I don't know how I got back here."

"You needed a break from your boss," Katie said.

"Carl?" Gilbert said. He frowned. "Yeah, he was coming down pretty hard on me. At least I think he was. It's hard to remember. Everything's a little fuzzy."

"He wasn't being fair," Katie told Gilbert. "You fixed the booth. You made it so people had a chance to win a prize . . ."

"I did WHAT?" Gilbert asked. He stopped for a minute. "Yeah, I guess I did do that. But *why*?"

"Because rigging games isn't nice," Katie said. "And it isn't fun for anyone. Besides, everyone stopped coming to your booth even though it had the best prizes because they saw that it was impossible to win."

"That's the way Carl wants it," Gilbert explained to her.

"Carl's not very nice," Katie said.

Gilbert laughed. "That's for sure. But he's my boss. And he's probably ready to kill me." He frowned. "I guess I better get back there. I can't spend all day just hanging out in a boneyard."

"That reminds me," Katie said. "What exactly is a boneyard?"

"It's where carnival workers take our breaks," Gilbert said. "Although, it's not actually back here near the dumpsters. We have a trailer in the parking lot with sodas and snacks. I wonder why I didn't just go there."

Because the magic wind didn't know about the boneyard trailer in the parking lot, that's why. But she didn't tell Gilbert that.

"I gotta go," Gilbert said. "No sense making Carl any madder than he already is—if that's even possible. You can hang out here if you want. Although I don't know what kind of kid would want to hang out by the garbage all afternoon when there's a carnival going on."

Katie agreed. She definitely wanted to go on rides and eat popcorn. Unfortunately, the magic wind kept changing her plans. And in the contest between Katie and the magic wind, there was no contest. It was rigged. The wind always won!

Chapter 16

"Hey, when are you going to open this booth?"

"My kid wants a teddy bear, let me shoot some darts!"

"Yo, are there any green bears left?"

Katie looked over at the booth and saw that the line was even longer now.

Just then, Carl spotted Katie and Gilbert and came running up to them.

"Oh, so you decided to come back" he said. "Why'd you go and leave me alone here? These people are like animals I had to close the booth."

"That's because this booth has the best prizes," Katie said. "And now that people see they have a chance at winning, they want to play."

"Who's the kid?" Carl asked Gilbert.

"I'm Katie," she told him. "And I think what Gilbert did here is great."

"Yeah, well, you're not the one giving away all those stuffed animals," Carl sneered.

"I'm not the one getting all the money from these people, either," Katie pointed out. "You are."

"Katie's right, Carl," Gilbert said. "These customers have a lot of cash. They'll fill my whole possum gut in a heartbeat."

"But what about the cost of giving away all those bears?" Carl asked.

"Those toys are not as expensive as you say, and you know it!" Gilbert said.

"Besides, not everyone wins," Katie pointed out. "So you fill your possum gut real fast." Katie smiled. She was starting to understand the lingo.

Gilbert nodded. "She's right," he said. "This booth wasn't making much alfalfa—until people started winning."

Carl thought for a minute. "You're pretty smart for a kid," he told Katie. "I guess we can try it this way—for a while. See how it goes." He moved out of the way. "Go ahead, Gil. Open your booth."

"Yea!" Katie cheered, running toward the booth. "This game's going to be fun." She reached into her pocket. But before she could hand over a dollar for some darts, she heard a familiar voice.

"THERE YOU ARE!"

Katie whipped around and saw Suzanne coming toward her with a half-eaten candy apple in each hand.

"I've been looking all over for you, Katie," Suzanne said. She was talking really, *really* fast. "I've been to the mechanical bull. But no Katie. And the Ferris wheel. But no Katie. And the whip. But no Katie. The carousel and . . ."

"Whoa! Slow down," Katie said. She looked at the half-eaten candy apples in Suzanne's hands. "How many of those things have you had?"

"I don't know, seven, eight . . . maybe twelve," Suzanne said. "What does it matter?" She stopped and looked at the money in Katie's hand. "Can I borrow a dollar? I need to get another candy apple. Mmmm, so delicious."

"Maybe that's enough," Katie said. Suzanne seemed really, really hyper. "I mean, you don't want to be all crazy during the Junior Miss Candy Apple Contest, and right now . . ."

"That's why I was looking for you!" Suzanne interrupted her. "The contest. It's starting soon. You have my glitter. I need that now. I need lots and lots and lots of glitter. Oh, and I need you in the crowd to cheer really, really loudly for me. A lot louder than you cheer for Emma. Judges like when people cheer. I like when people cheer. So come on!"

And with that, Suzanne sped back down the midway and toward the band shell where the contest was being held. Nothing moved as fast as a sugar-fueled Suzanne Lock.

Unless of course it was the magic wind. That moved pretty quickly, too. Katie only hoped Suzanne didn't spin out of control in quite the same way. Because that would be *sooo* not good.

Chapter 17

"Are we late?" Becky asked as she and Jeremy hurried over to where Katie was standing. Katie was near the band shell waiting for the Junior Miss Candy Apple Contest to start.

Becky was carrying a big blue bear in her arms.

"You didn't . . . ," Katie began to ask Jeremy.

"Uh-uh," Jeremy assured her. "All I won was this." He held up a plush kitten with soft black fur. It looked a lot like his own cat, Lucky. "I popped a balloon with my first dart!"

"I won my bear," Becky said proudly. "It took a lot of darts, and I had to wait in line a long time, but I did it!"

Katie smiled. She had been right. People were spending lots of money at the balloon-dartboard booth.

"I was so excited," Becky continued. "It took forever to find Jeremy and show him my bear. But I did!"

There was no getting away from Becky. Poor Jeremy.

"Hey, did Suzanne fall flat on her face yet?" Kevin asked as he, Kadeem, and Andrew joined them. Kevin was carrying a big red ribbon.

"Wow! You won second prize for your tomato, huh?" Katie asked him. "Sorry I missed it. I was on my way over but then . . ." Katie stopped mid-sentence. She wasn't sure what to say next. She couldn't tell Kevin that she was on her way over to see him when a magic wind started blowing.

Kevin said, "The guy who won first prize grew a tomato the size of a pumpkin. But I like this ribbon better. It's tomato red!"

"And now you can eat your tomato," Jeremy pointed out.

Kevin smiled. "Already did," he said with a grin.

"Ooooh." Andrew moaned. "Don't say *tomato*."

The kids all laughed.

"*Shhh . . . ,*" Becky whispered suddenly. "It's starting."

Just then, Slim Jim McQueen came onstage followed by the girls who had entered the Junior Miss Candy Apple Contest. They were all wearing matching candy apple red T-shirts that said SWEET AS A CANDY APPLE. The shirts were really cute, but Katie knew Suzanne probably hated wearing it. Suzanne always liked to be dressed differently than anyone else.

Emma looked really cute standing up there on the stage. She had a big red bow at the top of her long brown ponytail and just a touch of shiny red lip gloss on her lips. Katie guessed the lip gloss was Lacey's idea. Emma wasn't a lip gloss kind of girl.

Suzanne was standing on the other side of

the stage, as far from Emma as she could get. Actually, Suzanne wasn't exactly standing. It was more like she was dancing around—moving back and forth from one foot to the other and swinging her arms.

"What's with Suzanne?" Jeremy asked Katie.

"Twelve sugary candy apples," Katie told him.

Jeremy laughed. "That explains why her teeth are pink."

"Welcome to the Junior Miss Candy Apple Contest," Slim Jim McQueen said to the crowd. "One of these little ladies behind me will soon be crowned Junior Miss Candy Apple and get to ride in the parade at the end of the day."

"Oooh! I just love parades!" Suzanne squealed. She jumped up and down excitedly.

All the other contestants turned and stared at her. Suzanne stopped jumping and went back to jiggling around. She just couldn't keep still.

Slim Jim McQueen laughed. "Well, before we can have a parade, we have to have a contest.

Let's meet each of our contestants."

The first girl walked up to the microphone. She smiled at the crowd, flipped her long blond hair behind her, and gave a little wave. It seemed like she'd done this many times before.

"Hi there. I'm Cassie O'Dell," the blond girl said. "I love county fairs because I get to experience things I don't normally get to, like milking goats and cows and meeting all the wonderful people who run the rides and the games." She smiled at Slim Jim. "And real cowboys, too."

"Well, thank you, little lady," Slim Jim said. "Everyone, let's hear it for Cassie O'Dell."

Emma was next. She walked up to the microphone and said, "My name is Emma Weber. I'm at the fair with my sister and my three brothers. I like being in this contest because this is the first time I've done something all by myself all day."

Everyone in the crowd laughed. They thought Emma was making a joke. But Katie knew better. Emma had obviously had enough of taking care of her younger brothers.

"My name is Sandy Bleeker," the next contestant said into the microphone. "I've been coming to this carnival ever since I was a baby . . ."

As Sandy spoke, Katie glanced over at Suzanne. She was hopping around from one foot to the other, but now she was tapping her stomach with one hand and twirling her braid around and around with the other. And it looked like she was singing to herself. Suzanne had definitely had eleven too many candy apples.

"And now we'll hear from Suzanne Lock." A few minutes later, Slim Jim McQueen was finally announcing Suzanne.

Suzanne opened her lips wide and shot the crowd a big, pink-toothed smile. Then she started to walk toward the microphone. Only she wasn't doing her usual model-y walk. This time she was sort of running and dancing her way across the stage.

"Does Suzanne look green to you?" Becky asked Katie.

Jeremy, Andrew, Becky, and Kevin all laughed. But Katie didn't. Suzanne looked *terrible*.

Suzanne stared out at the crowd. She smiled again, only this grin seemed a little shaky. "My name is Suzanne Lock," she said. "I'm a fashion mod—"

BLEHHHH!

Before Suzanne could finish her speech, red,

gooey gunk exploded from her mouth. It looked like a volcano of candy apple lava erupting.

"She's puking!" Kadeem laughed. "Oh man, this is classic."

Suzanne clapped her hand over her mouth. Her eyes bugged. She started to run off the stage.

BLEHHHH!

Slim Jim McQueen jumped out of the way. The other contestants took giant steps back. One of them pinched her nose.

BLEHHHH!

"There she goes again!" Kevin laughed even harder. "Hey! You think she learned *that* at modeling school?"

Chapter 18

"That contest wasn't fair at all," Suzanne said a little while later as she and some of the other kids walked through the fairgrounds. "Cassie O'Dell has been doing pageants since she was a baby. She had a real advantage."

"Yeah, she also didn't puke onstage," Kadeem joked. "That's a definite advantage."

Some of the other kids laughed. But not Katie. Suzanne felt bad enough about what had happened. She didn't want to make her feel worse.

"I can't help it if I got a stomachache," Suzanne told Kadeem. "It must have been something I ate."

"Yeah, like twelve candy apples," Kevin said. Suzanne didn't answer.

"How about we go on the tilt-a-whirl," Kevin suggested.

Suzanne's face got that green look again. She gripped her stomach. "I don't think so."

"Me neither," Andrew agreed. "I still have all that P-I-E in my belly."

Katie giggled. She figured he was spelling the word so his stomach couldn't hear.

"How about we go on the froghopper?" Emma suggested.

Andrew and Suzanne both shook their heads.

"Too much bouncing," Andrew said.

"How about the Ferris wheel?" Katie pointed to the giant wheel in the middle of the fairgrounds. "That's pretty calm."

"The Ferris wheel sounds perfect," Suzanne said.

"Great," Katie said. "From up there, you can see everything."

The kids hurried over to the Ferris wheel.

"There's four people to a car," the ticket taker said.

"I'll go in your car, Jeremy," Becky said. "We can sit real, real close and hold our stuffed animals on our laps."

"Oh man." Jeremy groaned. He did not look happy about being stuck with Becky.

"How about girls in one car and boys in the other," Katie said quickly.

"Yeah, sounds great!" Jeremy said. He gave Katie a grateful smile. "You girls take this green car. We'll wait for the next one."

"Fine with me," Suzanne said. She crawled into the green car. Katie got in after her.

A few minutes later as the green car moved slowly around the giant circle, Katie looked down at the fairgrounds.

"Hey, is that Mrs. Derkman riding the mechanical bull?" Emma asked.

"I think so," Katie said. "That's the big sun hat with the flowers she was wearing during the flower judging."

"Did her roses win?" Emma asked Katie.

"Uh, I don't think so," was all Katie said.

Suzanne looked to her left. "There's the midway," she said. "And the carousel. Let's go on that next."

Before Katie could answer, she felt something blowing on her back. It was a cool breeze—a way-too-familiar cool breeze. Oh no! Not the magic wind. Not here, not now. *Not in front of all of her friends.*

"I wish I'd brought a sweater," Emma remarked. "It's kind of windy up here."

Phew. If Emma felt the wind, too, then it couldn't be the magic wind. It had to be a regular, run-of-the-mill, not switcherooing kind of wind. This was the kind of wind you felt when you were at the top of a Ferris wheel, overlooking a county fair with your best friends. And there was no better wind than that!

About the Author

Nancy Krulik is the author of more than 150 books for children and young adults, including three *New York Times* best sellers. She lives in New York City with her husband, composer Daniel Burwasser, and their children, Amanda and Ian. When she's not busy writing the *Katie Kazoo, Switcheroo* series, Nancy loves swimming, reading, and going to the movies.

About the Illustrators

John & Wendy have illustrated all of the *Katie Kazoo* books, but when they're not busy drawing Katie and her friends, they like to paint, take photographs, travel, and play music in their rock 'n' roll band. They live and work in Brooklyn, New York.